This edition published by Parragon Books Ltd in 2016 and distributed by

Parragon Inc.
440 Park Avenue South, 13th Floor
New York, NY 10016
www.parragon.com

Copyright © Parragon Books Ltd 2013-2016

Written by David Bedford
Edited by Laura Baker
Production by Jonathon Wakeham

Illustrated by Susie Poole
Designed by Alex Dimond and Duch Egg Blue

ISBN 978-1-4748-6276-9

Printed in China

You're a **BIG** Sister

PaRragon

Bath · New York · Cologne · Melbourne · Delhi
Hong Kong · Shenzhen · Singapore

You're going to be a big sister!
And that's so lucky for you ...

Babies LOVE their big sisters

and all the smart things that they do.

Big sisters know
babies like quiet,
so just smile
and whisper, "Hello."

Big sisters are really good helpers.
Let's all get ready … and go!

All babies are cute ...

fun ...

and cuddly,

but there are things a big sister
soon knows ...

Babies dribble ...

kick ...

and might even be sick ...

all over your clothes
and your toes!

Though they are so very tiny,
babies can make a BIG STINK ...

And when they're not feeling well ...

babies scream ...

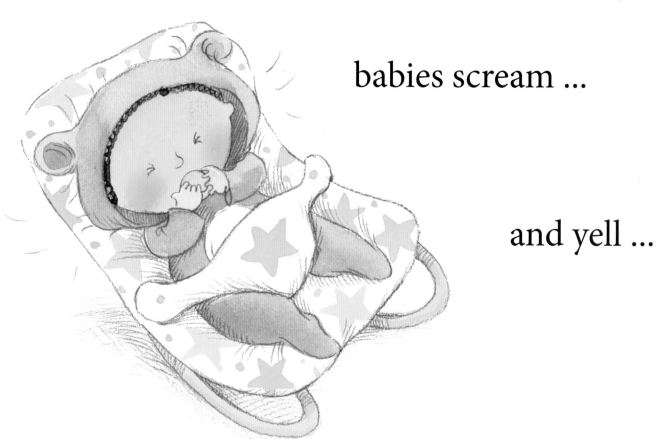

and yell ...

so loud you can't hear yourself think!

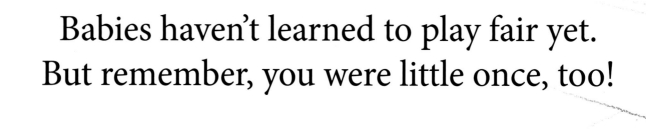

Babies haven't learned to play fair yet.
But remember, you were little once, too!

So be kind and share ...

Cuddle, play, and take care ...

And help them be clever like you!

When Mommy and Daddy are busy,
always know that they love you, too ...

And now that you're a big sister,

enjoy sharing with
somebody new!